TOXIC

"Greg groaned in his sleep as the reptile wound around him, twisting over his chest and neck. Its muscles slowly tightened – tighter and tighter … till Greg opened his eyes.

Choking from the weight on his throat, Greg felt jaws clamp on his head. Teeth dug into his ears. He smelt stinking breath seeping over his face.

As he tried to scream, no cry came – just a croak. "

TERROR
OF THE
SWAMP

Terror of the Swamp

by John Townsend
Illustrated by Dante Ginevra

Published by Ransom Publishing Ltd.
Radley House, 8 St. Cross Road, Winchester, Hampshire
SO23 9HX, UK
www.ransom.co.uk

ISBN   978 178127 719 5
First published in 2015

TERROR
OF THE
SWAMP

JOHN
TOWNSEND

ILLUSTRATED BY
DANTE GINEVRA

Ransom

CHAPTER 1

A massive snake slid through the swamp in the darkness. Its flicking tongue sensed prey; something warm and alive. Its fangs flashed in the moonlight.

Greg stirred in the tent. He slept soundly in the sticky night, with its croaking frogs and chirping crickets. He'd never been so tired. Hiking and canoeing through the jungle had worn him out.

His dad slept deeply too. Their camp fire was now just smoking ash in the clearing.

The snake slithered from the swamp. Its heavy body squelched through the mud, over tree roots, and zig-zagged past a canoe.

Seven metres of African rock python slid by the fire's ashes and into the tent. Its glistening tongue flicked faster and the cold eyes stared.

It slowly slipped around the sleeping boy. Scaly skin slid silently over his flesh … until its tongue brushed his cheek with a hiss.

Greg groaned in his sleep as the reptile wound around him, twisting over his chest and neck. Its muscles slowly tightened –

tighter and tighter … till Greg opened his eyes.

At first he thought he was tangled in a knotted sheet. But why was it moving? Why couldn't he wriggle free? Why couldn't he breathe?

Choking from the weight on his throat, Greg felt jaws clamp on his head. Teeth dug into his ears. He smelt stinking breath seeping over his face. As he tried to scream, no cry came – just a croak.

His dad stirred.

'Be quiet, Greg. You're having a bad dream. Go back to sleep.'

Once more, Greg tried to force a sound from his throat.

His dad grunted. 'Ssh. Get some rest. We've got a long day ahead. Settle down.'

A gurgle beside him in the blackness made his dad reach for his torch.

'I said stop your noise, Greg.'

With a click of the switch, light filled the tent. The beam pointed at where Greg's face should have been.

Instead of Greg's face, there were the gaping jaws of a python – with a ten year-old boy's head trapped inside. A thick, green body was crushing his ribs and squeezing air from his lungs.

His dad threw himself at the jaws. No amount of pulling could loosen them. Greg was locked in a vice-like grip.

The snake's body twisted even tighter round his neck, turning like a tightening screw.

Grabbing a can of insect spray from his kitbag, his dad squirted it at the snake's eyes. A spurt of stinging fluid hit its face.

The jaws instantly unlocked. Teeth tore across Greg's cheeks as the thrashing snake spat and hissed.

Ramming a kitbag at its jaws, Greg's dad fought to uncoil the other end. The louder he shouted, the more it loosened. He wrestled to unwind its writhing bulk with one hand. With the other he held the hissing head at arm's length.

At last Greg wriggled free, rolled to the edge of the tent and lay gasping. He gulped the damp, swampy air as his dad pushed the python's head into a sleeping bag.

When he'd bundled its whole body inside, he hurled the squirming sack into the night. They heard a splash in the darkness as the python slid back into the swamp.

It sank to the riverbed. But it moved no further. It had tasted blood. Warm human blood. The sort it craved.

Nothing would stop it now. Its reptile brain had reset. It was fixed on revenge.

It would return with the moon ... with back-up. Next time with extra force.

For the kill.

CHAPTER 2

The campfire crackled as a pot above it simmered.

'Drink this, Greg. My brew will make you feel better.'

With a bandage on his head, Greg sipped from a tin mug.

'Thanks, Dad. I'll be OK. Hey – when I asked to come on a jungle trek, I thought I'd see *wow* stuff – but not a snake's tonsils from the inside!'

His dad, whose name was Baron, sighed. 'When I did my SAS jungle training, we never saw a brute that size. That was the biggest rock python I've ever seen. I thought our main risk would be crocs, hippos and biting mozzies. This part of Africa has more surprises than I thought. The swamp stretches for hundreds of miles across Congo's rainforest.'

Greg sat in a daze, staring into the flames.

'I don't want to give up, Dad. I want to keep going. You've got a job to do. I'm glad you let me come with you. Don't let that stuff with the snake change anything.'

His dad put down his mug.

'You're a brave lad. Your mum didn't want me to bring you. Nor did my commanding officer. He said army work isn't for kids. I told him he didn't know my son. If anyone can help me find the missing explorers, you can.'

'Unless they've been eaten by that python's twin sister!' Greg smiled for the first time. 'How come you didn't bring lots more SAS men? More troops would be better at finding the guys we're looking for.'

Greg watched his dad prod the fire with a stick before sitting beside him.

'The thing is, Greg, I haven't told you all the facts. I guess now is the time. You see, it's safer to get through this jungle with only two of us. The more men, the more risks. More noise might wake the monsters.'

Greg stared in disbelief as his dad added, 'My commanding officer said he couldn't risk other men. Just me, of course! He said I was the best man for the job, as I know about jungles and their dangers. I'm mad with myself for messing up just now. I should have dealt with that snake quicker. Sorry, Greg.'

Before he could say more, a roar filled the night. A sudden rumble shook the trees.

Then deathly silence. The frogs stopped croaking and the crickets fell silent. Monkeys no longer shrieked in the moonlit treetops.

'What was that?' Greg gasped. 'It didn't sound like a lion or an elephant.'

'More likely an earth tremor. Mind you, jungle animals make weird noises under a full moon.' His dad paused before whispering,

'Unless it was the beast. The monster. A living dinosaur – known as *the beast that stops the river*. Or as the locals call it – *Mokele Mbembe*.'

'Don't wind me up, Dad. I've been wound up enough for one night!'

Baron smiled.

'It isn't a joke. Experts have come here looking for it for years. With all the dense tree-cover and deep lakes, not much can be seen from the air – even monsters. It's like looking for a needle in a sea of haystacks. Dan Reeves came out here last week to try and film it. He wanted to be the first star to make it to the middle of the swamp.'

'That guy off the TV? He's here?'

'Yeah – with a TV crew and his daughter. Three days ago they vanished. All contact lost. Nothing.

'That's why I got the call – in secret. The TV bosses fear the worst. Armed bandits can hide here. Or maybe one of the many quicksands got them. Or a killer disease, a man-eater or deadly thorns. It's our job to find them, Greg. Are you still up for this? It could get scary.'

Greg smiled again.

'Well it hasn't exactly been a picnic so far! But as I begged you to let me come with you, I can't get stressy now, can I? Anyway, you said you need me to climb trees and be a look-out. I'm much better than you at climbing trees. You always say I'm a super-ape!'

Before his dad could reply, a growl rose from the swamp. In the silence that followed, a blood-curdling shriek filled the night. It wasn't a monkey this time. There was no doubt about it.

It was the scream of a girl.

CHAPTER 3

'Who's there?'

Baron called across the swamp. He flashed his torch through the swirling mist that rolled over the soupy black water.

'Over there, Dad.' Greg pointed to where he heard a splash in the darkness.

They could see nothing, but heard a distant cry. It sounded like 'Help'.

'We'll take the canoe,' his dad said. He grabbed his rifle. 'I may need this.'

*****

The two-man canoe slipped through the reeds and into the mist. Greg sat in the back, paddling hard.

Baron stopped paddling now and again to listen and sweep his torch over the water.

He called, 'Where are you?'

Somewhere ahead they heard 'Here!'

Greg steered the canoe towards the voice. They peered through the steamy darkness. Nothing. Apart from the sound of ripples as the canoe sliced through the lake, the night

was eerily silent. Dark shapes loomed up from the moonlit water ahead.

'Stop paddling, Greg,' his dad said. 'It's a bank with trees and … '

He squinted at what he thought was a log floating past. Then he saw its green eyes. With a sudden thud and spray, the canoe spun as the crocodile struck.

Greg froze as his dad hit at the crocodile's jaws with his oar. The canoe lifted from the water and slammed against tree roots.

Greg clung on as they rocked from side to side. Baron pulled a rope from the canoe and fixed an end to a tree beside them. He quickly tied a loop in the other end as the crocodile swam towards them.

Greg feared it would smash the canoe to bits and drag them under. Once in its jaws, they wouldn't stand a chance. It would roll them over and over along the bed of the lake.

Baron aimed his lasso at the snout speeding towards them. As the nostrils rose from the water, he threw it. The loop slid over the crocodile's mouth and he yanked it shut.

Despite all the thrashing, the rope tightened and held. The reptile's jaws couldn't open and were firmly attached to the tree trunk. It would take a while for it to wriggle free.

Greg patted his dad's back as the muzzled crocodile tugged on its lead. But Greg hadn't seen what was above them in the torchlight.

His dad raised his rifle and took aim.

'Don't move. Stay very still.'

Looking up, Greg saw a girl clinging to a branch. But coiled around the branch above her was a shiny black mamba. The deadly snake was moving towards her hand.

Suddenly a shot ripped through the branches. The girl screamed as the snake fell. It dropped past her feet and splashed into the water below.

Lowering the rifle, Baron called, 'You're fine now. We'll help you. Don't worry. You'll be OK.'

He turned to Greg.

'That black mamba is the fastest and most deadly snake. One drop of its venom could kill all of us in minutes. That's super-toxic!'

They brought the canoe close to the tree and Greg scrambled up.

'I'm good with trees,' he said, taking hold of her arm.

'I'm rubbish,' she panted. 'But I'm worse with crocs. I don't know who you are, but am I glad to see you! Not that I can see in the dark. And you speak English. How lucky is that? You must be a knight in shining armour!'

'No – just a kid in a battered canoe.'

Soon the girl was sitting in the canoe being paddled back across the lake. Greg sat astride the canoe, his feet skimming the water.

The girl spoke very fast – she was still scared.

'I'm Em. That's short for Emelia. I'm twelve. My dad's Dan Reeves. Everyone knows who he is. But the thing is … '

She stopped talking and wiped her eyes.

'I'm really worried. We were having a great time back there, but he and his crew are in big danger. I just got away in time. I ran to get help but I got lost in the dark. It was so scary. If you hadn't rescued me just in time … '

The canoe steered towards a flickering light ahead. Their campfire still burned in the clearing.

As they all clambered up the bank, Em blurted, 'I've got to tell you. Please help. The thing is … what I've got to say is urgent. Life and death stuff. My dad's fate is in your hands.'

CHAPTER 4

Once more the campfire crackled as a pot simmered on top.

Baron stirred a mug.

'Drink this, Em. My brew will make you feel better.'

Greg sat beside her, with a muddy bandage still round his head. He smiled.

'In the last hour I've met two scary snakes, a huge croc and a girl up a tree.'

'I could be the most deadly,' she said. 'That's if you'll help me save my dad. It's high risk, but from what I've seen of you so far, I reckon you can do it.'

'You must tell us exactly what kind of danger your father is in,' Baron said calmly. 'I need to hear it as it is. And I guess the threat isn't from the beast they call Mokele Mbembe.'

'That's the living dinosaur we came to find – known as MM. We haven't seen it yet. The threat to my dad right now is from two men called Bryce and Edmon. They run a brutal poacher gang. They kill elephants and hack off their tusks.'

'Ivory is big money,' Baron sighed. 'I've seen how cruel some of the poachers are. They've wiped out elephants in parts of Congo.'

Em put her mug down and stared into the fire.

'I *so* wanted to come with Dad on this trip. No one has ever filmed MM before. Local people told us where they'd seen it, so we headed off through the jungle. We found dead hippos in the swamp, which our guide told us were killed by MM. We began filming – with me talking on camera – when suddenly the poacher gang ran out of the jungle. They shouted at us and waved their guns. They rounded us up, led us to a hut and tied us up. They thought we'd come to film them to get them arrested. They took our camera and phones and said they'd kill us if we tried to escape.'

'So how did you escape?' Greg asked.

'It was really weird,' she went on. 'When they heard my name is Emelia, the guy named Edmon went all twitchy. It was like he'd seen a ghost.'

'I think I know why,' Baron said. 'The word *Emela* scares local people. *Emela Ntouka* is another of the feared beasts round here. It means 'killer of elephants'.

'They say it's a huge creature that lives in the swamp. Emela Ntouka is said to attack elephants in water, with its long sharp horn. Local tribes dread meeting it face-to-face. It's meant to bring bad luck. The very name of the mythical beast is like a curse.'

Em smiled.

'So I'm like a curse round here! That must be why they gave me weird looks.

Then it got scary when an army of ants came through the camp. The men had to untie us fast or we'd have been eaten alive. We grabbed our phones, but I was the only one who got right away. I ran till it got dark. That's when I ran into that croc. I couldn't get a signal on my phone, so I'm lucky you found me. I'm so scared the poachers will hurt Dad and his three-man crew. Can you help find them?'

'Of course,' Baron said. 'That's why we came. I've heard about the man called Bryce. The police want him for lots of crimes, but they don't know what he looks like.'

'Mean and scary,' she said. 'He's got two fingers missing. He told us a tiger fish bit them off.'

'Tiger fish round here are worse than piranhas,' Baron warned. 'If they attack in the river, you've had it.'

He paced round the fire before adding, 'We need to get into action. I'll have to follow your tracks back to where you escaped. From there, I'll follow tracks to their new camp. Try your phone now. See if you can send your dad a text, just in case.'

Em shook her head.

'I've already tried. The signal is rubbish under all the trees. I don't even know if he's got his phone, or if it's charged.'

'Then allow me.'

Greg took the phone from her and ran to a tree trunk.

'It's time for Super-ape to get up there to the satellite. Up I go to the moon!'

He scrambled up into the branches, bathed in fiery tropical moonlight.

Swinging high above them he called down, 'Yeah – I've got a signal!'

He tapped in a text to Em's dad.
'Am safe. Help on way.'

Before he could send it, a text arrived.

'Men about to kill us. Love you 4 ever. Dad.'

CHAPTER 5

As soon as it was light, the canoe slipped through the silver mist across the lake.

When they reached the far bank, Baron tied the canoe to the rope left behind by the crocodile.

With birds screeching in the trees, Em tried to retrace her steps from the night before.

They pushed their way through the undergrowth – Greg's dad noting each bent leaf, broken twig or footprint.

He tracked his way through the jungle easily, with Em and Greg following close behind.

*****

At last they came to a clearing with mud huts and a fenced pen. Flies buzzed over scattered bones.

'This was where they kept a goat,' Em pointed.

'It looks like ants stripped it to the bone,' Baron said. 'Army ants march through these forests in their millions. They eat anything that moves – even people, if they can't get away. Even elephants run from them. That goat didn't stand a chance.'

Looking at the ground around the deserted camp, they could see which way the poachers and their prisoners had escaped. Once more, Baron led the way through the jungle.

'At least a bunch of men carrying elephant tusks leave an easy path to follow.'

By midday, after a drenching downpour followed by a steamy trek through hot mud, Greg pointed at a flash of red moving through the trees ahead.

'Someone in a T shirt,' he whispered. They hid and watched.

'That's one of the gang,' Em said. 'He's nasty.'

Baron peered through binoculars from the bushes.

'He's collecting wood, so I guess there's a campfire nearby. We must be near their base.'

They followed the man as he headed off through the jungle. He joined others cutting trees by a stream.

After wading through a swamp full of frogs, they came to the edge of a clearing. Wisps of wood smoke drifted through the bushes, from where they could see shelters made of sticks and palm leaves. A fire blazed by a pile of tusks and animal hides. Two men with rifles sat in the sun, keeping watch.

'I need to get past those guards to see what's inside the shelters,' Baron whispered. 'It's not safe for you to come with me. Besides, I don't want you to see what might be there.'

Em didn't have to ask what he meant. She already feared they were too late to save her dad. She'd been trying not to think the worst.

'You take my rucksack, Greg,' he went on. 'Have a drink and a rest.'

He paused before adding quietly, 'If anything happens to me ... get straight back to our camp across the lake. Wait there till help arrives. But don't worry, Greg. I won't be long.'

After a silent high-five, Greg watched his dad sneak off through the shadows.

He turned to Em and smiled.

'If anyone can get your dad back, my dad can. Fancy a drink?'

He looked in the rucksack with a smile. 'You'd better stand clear when I open this can of Coke. The last one almost exploded after it was shaken up so much.'

Em was about to take the can when she felt cold steel against her cheek. She turned with a gasp – and stared down the barrel of a gun.

With one finger on the trigger, a man with two other fingers missing stared down at them.

'You're dead,' he growled.

CHAPTER 6

With their hands tied behind them around separate trees, Greg and Em faced the man they knew was Bryce.

'Don't even think about shouting for help,' he snapped. 'One sound and I'll shoot.'

He pointed his rifle at them, his eyes raging.

'I hate kids. I hate anyone who gets in my way.'

He stared at Em. 'I should have killed you before. Who's the boy?'

Greg spoke. 'A friend.'

The man yelled, 'I didn't ask you.'

His nose almost touched Greg's as he hissed, 'You only speak when I say. What's in the bag?'

He looked at the rucksack in the grass.

Greg stuttered, 'Not much. Drink and stuff.'

Still pointing his gun at them, the man picked it up.

'You won't want it. I'm going to take you to where the others are about to die.'

He turned to glare at Em.

'Your father and his friends won't last long. Nor will you. They're lying in the sun – stretched out. I've pegged them to the ground in the path of those army ants.'

He pointed across the clearing to what at first looked like a rippling stream. It was a heaving line of ants – millions of wriggling legs shining in the sunlight.

'They're already on the move,' Bryce sneered. 'On their way to eat them alive. The whole ant army will be there in ten minutes. So will you. You're their dinner.

They always take the same route and always eat all flesh in their path.'

With a chilling cackle, he reached into Greg's bag and took out a can.

'It's thirsty work watching kids get eaten alive.'

He ripped off the ring-pull and swore as the Coke fizzed over him in a shower of froth. Slamming the can in the mud, his eyes raged more than ever.

'You'll pay for that.'

He grabbed Greg by the throat and was about to strike him when Em squealed.

'Look out! Behind you!'

Bryce hissed in fury.

'Do you take me for a fool? I'd never fall for that.'

She didn't give up.

'The ants are coming!'

A river of ants was gushing towards them – a seething mass, scrambling nearer and nearer. They tumbled over each other in their rush to find the sugar in the Coke.

Bryce stepped back, raised his gun to take aim at Greg, as the first ants scampered over his boots. He looked down in horror as hundreds of tiny jaws tore at his ankles.

He stamped and ran.

'I can run – but you won't. They'll swarm all over you.'

But they didn't. Instead, they all turned to chase him.

The can on the ground was a writhing clump of thirsty ants. They scurried over the sticky sweet trail to the screaming man covered in the same sugary liquid. They were crawling over his body as he ran to the river. He dived into the water to get them off him.

Splashing and screaming madly, he was suddenly dragged right under. The water bubbled red as he thrashed and shrieked, until he disappeared below the churning water for the last time.

As the squad of soldier ants marched on along the river bank, Em gasped.

'Did you see that? Ants wouldn't get him in the river, would they?'

Greg could only stare.

'There's something else in that river. Something big. I saw huge teeth. Whatever it is, it's eaten him.'

Pushing up with his feet, Greg slowly climbed the tree trunk. By shuffling short steps then sliding his tied hands upwards, he reached to where the trunk was thinner.

As the rope got looser, he was able to slip his hands free. He jumped down to untie Em and found her phone in the bag.

'Yay! I've got a text from Dad,' she yelled. 'They're OK! Your dad found them and set them free. He's taking them back to your camp across the lake.'

She was so excited that she didn't read the next part.

'C U there. Get back quick. Don't cross lake. Go round on land. Thick mist over water. Something big in swamp. Coming nearer. Take care. Dad X'

When Greg read it, he sighed.

'I don't want to scare you,' he said grimly, 'but the signal's gone again. I haven't got a clue which way to go. I've got no idea how to get back. We're stuck.'

CHAPTER 7

'It may take a girl's skill to get us out of here,' Em grinned. 'Even though you saved a damsel in distress, she must now save you and get us back.'

'We'll never be able to follow our tracks like my dad can,' Greg sighed.

Em held up her phone.

'Technology to the rescue. I'll scroll my location history and get the GPS of the call you made up the tree back there. The satnav app will point us to the exact spot. If we need to refresh the signal, you'll just have to climb a tree!'

*****

After scrambling up trees, wading through knee-deep mud and hacking through dense jungle, Greg slumped to his knees by the lake.

'At last. Our camp is just over the water, through the mist.'

Em looked at her phone.

'According to the satnav, we just have to walk a couple of miles along the shore and we'll be back.'

Sinister noises bubbled and gurgled inside the fog. An elephant trumpeted somewhere across the water. Growls and rumbles echoed through the trees.

As they plodded on, Greg felt sure they were being watched. It was as if eyes were following them from deep inside the churning brown mist.

*****

By the time they staggered back to camp, Greg's dad had already built shelters by the tent and a campfire was blazing. Em's dad cooked meat on it, but no one dared ask what it was. His crew smiled as hugs and cheers went on and on.

'I've already contacted my commanding officer,' Greg's dad cheered. 'They're sending in a seaplane to pick us up downriver tomorrow.'

Em looked across the lake.

'A shame the poachers took our camera. We might still catch a glimpse of MM if we're lucky. I so hope it's really out there.'

Through the mist a dark shape stirred. Ripples spread over the water and waves lapped against the banks ... as the moon began to rise in the darkening sky.

*****

Much later, Greg stood at the edge of the vast lake, peering into the golden moonlit mist.

Behind him, in the glow of the campfire, his dad served steaming drinks. Everyone was laughing. The famous Dan Reeves told stories. Em sang songs and the night was alive with croaking frogs and chirping crickets once more.

Greg felt a warm glow inside. He had helped his dad rescue some great people. Despite all the scares, their trip had turned out alright in the end.

Suddenly he glimpsed a murky shape through the parting mist. It moved across the water with a deep growl, then vanished with a splash.

He was sure he'd seen glowing red eyes just metres away. A rumble shook the ground beneath him. Perhaps it was just another earth tremor – or maybe only his imagination.

Greg smiled. He was always getting told off for imagining things.

For a split-second he even thought he saw a man emerge through the mist. A mean-looking man, covered in mud and holding an AKA rifle. A man with a wet face and eyes full of hate …

'I've come to kill you,' the man croaked. 'I followed your tracks. That girl put a curse on my friends. I found their smashed rowing boat drifting on the lake. The beast got them.'

'Who are you?' Greg gulped.

'Edmon. Bryce was my best friend. I've come for revenge. I don't care who or what I kill. I destroy elephants – and any people who get in my way. Like you. I'm here to shoot you all.'

Greg stared at the man in horror … as a shadow slowly rose out of the water.

A giant snake slid up from black slime, its huge body pushing through the reeds. But this was far bigger than the python he'd met the night before. This was a reptile from another world. A primeval monster.

As its enormous head rose higher, Greg gasped in disbelief.

Fangs flashed, cold eyes stared and a massive body squelched over tree roots towards the man's kicking legs. Suddenly the jaws opened and it struck. Teeth ripped into the man's foot.

Sliding backwards in the mud, he stared up with bloodcurdling squeals. His gun spun away into the river as he thrashed helplessly.

The more he struggled, the tighter the jaws gripped his leg. With each gulp, the snake's fangs chewed higher up the man's body.

From the waist down he'd already disappeared inside the gaping mouth.

Greg stared, unable to move. The terror of the night before froze him again, numbing his brain. He could only watch in total shock as the crunching jaws crushed the man's ribs.

When only Edmon's head and arms poked from its mouth, the reptile slowly turned towards the river. Gulping more of its wriggling prey, it squelched down the bank and plunged below the murky water.

Silence. The night fell deathly still.

Greg blinked into the darkness. Behind him, the singing continued in the firelight.

Then came laughter as someone told another story.

But Greg had his own story to tell now.

Maybe they wouldn't believe him. He took a deep breath, turned slowly and quietly walked towards the flames.

He'd tell them. He'd tell them everything. He'd tell them the story he'd never forget.

He'd tell everyone of the terror out there ... still moving beneath the water ...

The real terror of the swamp.

THE EMELA-NTOUKA

The Emela-Ntouka is a legendary African creature whose name means 'killer of the elephants'.

Its body is supposed to be to be similar in shape and appearance to a rhino, but about the size of an African elephant. It has one long horn, is brownish-grey in colour and makes a noise like a low growl.

People say these creatures live in the vast swamps and lakes that are part of the Congo River in Africa. They live on their own and eat swamp weeds and other plants.

THE MOKELE-MBEMBE

The Mokele-mbembe is another African mythical creature. Its name means 'one who stops the flow of the rivers'.

It is said to live in the Congo River, like the Emela-Ntouka, and prefers deep water to swamps.

It has a body similar to an elephant or rhino but with a smaller head, a very long neck and a tail like a dinosaur.

Some tribes in Africa believe the Mokele-mbembe is a spirit rather than a real flesh and blood creature.

DANGEROUS ANTS

Many kinds of ant are capable of stinging, biting and spraying harmful chemicals, but very few ants can kill humans.

The venom of the Jack Jumper Ant in Australia can cause allergic reactions which can lead to deaths, but this is very rare.

There are over 200 different kinds of army ant. Most ants build permanent nests to live in but army ants are always on the move. They are constantly travelling in order to hunt large amounts of prey for the millions of ants in their colonies. So army ants build a new nest almost every day, at dusk.

THE TITANOBOA

The rock python is Africa's largest snake. It lives in swamps, grassland or forests – and is well-known for being aggressive. This powerful boa constrictor can reach 7 metres long and weigh 90kg. Its massive bulk means it can easily prey on monkeys, warthogs, antelopes and even crocodiles.

The titanoboa (it means 'titanic boa') was a true monster snake, twice the size of an African rock python (about the length and weight of a school bus!). It probably died out 5 million years after the dinosaurs became extinct. This giant snake would slither under water towards its prey then snap its massive jaws onto its victim. It could easily swallow whole a large crocodile.

Could there really be a giant prehistoric snake in the African Congo today?

In 1959, a Belgian pilot flew a helicopter over the swamps of Congo and reported seeing a giant snake about 15 metres long. When he flew down to take a closer look, he said the huge reptile lunged at his helicopter.

Impossible? Vast areas of the African Congo still remain unexplored.

A rock python attacks a goat.

The Black Mamba

The black mamba is a real African snake. It is the most dangerous and feared snake in Africa. Its venom is highly poisonous and is one of the fastest-acting in the world; its bite can kill an adult human in 20 minutes! No wonder its bite is known as 'the kiss of death'.

Like most snakes, the black mamba will normally only attack a person if it is threatened or provoked. It is shy and secretive and tends to use its great speed to escape attacks rather than to hunt prey.

T☢XIC

MORE GREAT TOXIC READS

Action-packed adventure stories featuring jungles, swamps, deserted islands, robots, space travel, zombies, computer viruses and monsters from the deep.

How many have you read?

CRASH LAND EARTH

by Jonny Zucker

Jed and his friends are setting out on a trip to Mars. But their spaceship is in trouble and they are forced to crash-land back on Earth. But nothing is quite as it should be. Jed and his fellow explorers find themselves in a race against time to save planet Earth.

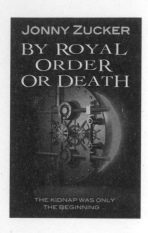

BY ROYAL ORDER OR DEATH

by Jonny Zucker

Miles is a member of the Royal Protection Hub, whose job is to protect the Royal family. When Princess Helena is kidnapped, Miles uncovers a cunning and dangerous plot. Miles must use all his skills to outwit the kidnappers and save the princess's life.

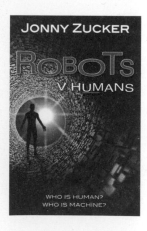

ROBOTS V HUMANS

by Jonny Zucker

Nico finds himself with five other kids – all his age. None of them can remember anything from their past. Then they are told that three of them are human and the other three are robots. Can Nico find out who is human and who are the robots?

MORE GREAT TOXIC READS

ZOMBIE CAMP

by Jonny Zucker

Arjun and Kev are at summer camp. It's great – there's lots to do and places to explore. But after a while Arjun and Kev begin to suspect that nothing is quite as it seems. Can they avoid the terrible fate that awaits them?

VIRUS 21

by Jonny Zucker

A new computer virus is rapidly spreading throughout the world. It is infecting everything, closing down hospitals, airports and even the internet. Can Troy and Macy find the hackers before the whole world shuts down?

John Townsend has been writing all sorts since he was a child – and he says he still hasn't grown up! John writes both fiction stories and non-fiction, and he loves writing for people who don't think they like books. (He always surprises them!)

John used to be a teacher, but now writes full-time. He is a recognised National Literacy Trust 'Reading Champion'.